with **Finn** and
His **Brother** Shane

By Margaret Mulvey

ILLUSTRATED BY Gil Balbuena Jr

To order additional copies of this book, contact:
Xlibris Corporation
1-888-795-4274
www.Xlibris.com
Orders@Xlibris.com

For My Grandson Shane,

Think The Impossible!
Believe ImpossibleThings!
Be happy and always be kind.

With much Love,
Your Mimi

4

Wow! here's our boy Finn again
And he's been learning lots of tricks
And what do you think makes him smile?
A young brother's been added to the mix!

Finn' brothers name is SHANE
And he's as handsome as can be
They play together, and have good times
As everyone can see.

Last week they went on a camping trip
With Mommy and Daddy and Uncle Bill
They set up the tent..had something to eat
Then the boys took a walk up the hill.

Well they climbed and they climbed
Then Finn ran ahead
And that's when Shane saw the BEAR!
Shane yelled, "Hey Finn, LOOK OUT!!!
But Finn was too far away to hear

Shane had his orange whistle
round about his neck
So he blew it as hard as he could
Finn turned around and saw the BEAR
And chased that bear into the woods!!!!

Finn ran down the hill really FAST
And when he reached his brother
He grinned a happy smile
From one end of his mouth to the other..

"Thanks Shane", said Finn
"You were really there for me"
You're the best brother, Shane
That ever there could be"

So let's try to remember
To watch out, each for the other..
All our family, all our friends
But especially ..our BROTHER!!!!

P.S. And/or a Sister!

THE END

CPSIA information can be obtained
at www.ICGtesting.com
Printed in the USA
LVHW070334280519
619258LV00012B/616/P